MOOKI
and the
TOO-PROUD PEACOCK

Written by
Kari Smalley Gibson *with* Gary Smalley
Illustrated by Barbara Spurll

Zonderkidz

Zonderkidz™

www.zonderkidz.com

Mooki and the Too-Proud Peacock
ISBN 0-310-70303-4
Copyright © 2002 by Kari Smalley Gibson
Illustrations copyright © 2002 by Barbara Spurll

Requests for information should be addressed to:
Zonderkidz, Grand Rapids, Michigan 49530

Editor: Gwen Ellis
Art Direction: Jody Langley

Printed in China
02 03 04 05/HK/ 4 3 2 1

Dedicated to...

Michael and Hannah
You are a gift from God....I love you!!!

**Taylor, Cole, Madalyn, Reagan, Garrison,
Kirsten, Alyssa** and **Abigail**
Aunti Kiki loves you all so much!

Illustrator's Dedication

To David for your wisdom, love, and commitment.

And to Welland and Victoria—you delight
and inspire me every day!

Payton Peacock stood in front of his classroom as proud as…well, you know…a peacock.

"Pharaoh," said Miss Taylor. "The word is pharaoh."

"Pharaoh. P-H-A-R…A…O—H. Pharaoh." Payton spelled carefully.

"That's right, Payton!" Miss Taylor was truly excited. "That's a very hard word, but you spelled it correctly. Congratulations! You win the spelling bee today, Payton."

Payton cocked his head this way and he cocked his head that way to make sure he had everyone's full attention. "I did it. I won the spelling bee. I'm the best." He stretched tall, carefully arranged each of his long tail feathers, and strutted back to his seat.

Mooki Beaver and the rest of the forest critters looked at each other and rolled their eyes. *That Payton*, thought Mooki. *He always brags.*

"It's time for recess," Miss Taylor said. "Run on out to play for a little while. "When you come back in I will have a special announcement."

The forest critters had no sooner gone out the schoolhouse door than it began to rain. Then it poured rain. Mooki got out his umbrella and just as he pushed it up, *whoosh*; Payton jerked it right out of his hand.

"Hey," yelled Mooki. "What do you think you're doing?"

"Well, you wouldn't want me to get my gorgeous iridescent feathers wet, would you?"

"Grrr," said Mooki.

Recess ended, and the critters hurried back into the classroom to hear Miss Taylor's announcement.

"Hedge Hollow's summer parade is next Saturday. Every year our class has a float in the parade. I would love for everyone to dress up and ride on the float," Miss Taylor told them. "It's lots of fun."

"Wowsy!" cheered Mooki. "What kind of dressing up should we do?"

"All you have to do is create a hat using nature's treasures. Use leaves, sticks, flowers, rocks, feathers, berries ... anything you like as long as it can be found in the great outdoors.

"Payton, what will you make?" asked Miss Taylor. "People are still talking about the hat you made last year."

Payton preened a bit and then said in a very snooty voice, "Weellll, last year I found some *magnificent* pine cones. I strung them together with long grass to make a wide brim on my hat. It took days and days. Great works of art take time to create, you know."

The other critters moaned and scowled. *Payton is always bragging and trying to impress everybody,* thought Mooki. *Why does he do that? Doesn't he realize it makes us all feel bad about ourselves?*

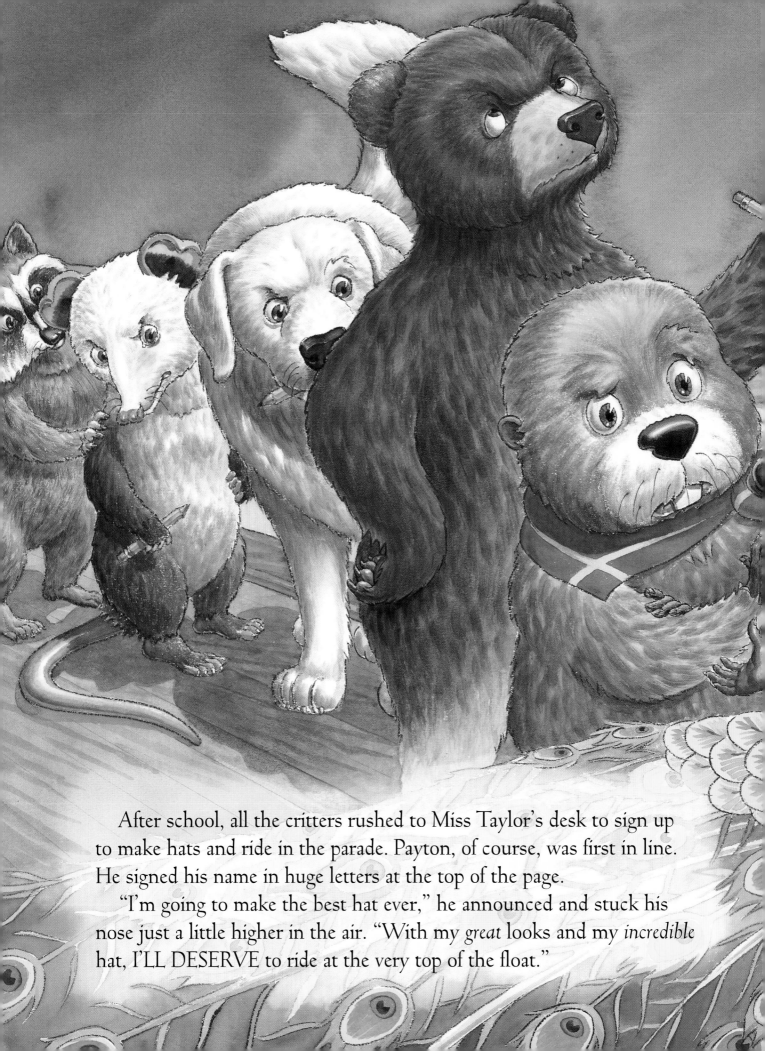

After school, all the critters rushed to Miss Taylor's desk to sign up to make hats and ride in the parade. Payton, of course, was first in line. He signed his name in huge letters at the top of the page.

"I'm going to make the best hat ever," he announced and stuck his nose just a little higher in the air. "With my *great* looks and my *incredible* hat, I'LL DESERVE to ride at the very top of the float."

Mooki and the other critters just frowned as Payton strutted away.

"He can be sooo snobby sometimes," grumbled Gibby Bear.

"Tell me about it," Mikey the dog growled. "He thinks he's the best at everything."

"Well, he is pretty good at most everything," Hannah Hedgehog whispered shyly.

Mooki gave Hannah a little hug. "You're right about that, Hannah. The problem is he keeps reminding us of it! All the time!"

"I just wish he'd stop being so stuck up," Mikey whined. "If Payton's hat is going to outshine all of our creations, what's the point of trying?"

Then Mooki spoke up, "Hey! Wait a minute! Making hats is supposed to be fun. It's not about being best. It's about doing something fun together. We all get to ride on the float. Let's just forget about old Payton. Let's just have fun!"

"Right!" chirped Gregory in his cheeriest chipmunk voice. "Let's do what Miss Taylor said and celebrate the wonder of nature." He thought for a minute and then said, "NUTS! Can you think of anything more wonderful than a hat full of nuts?"

The critters laughed and then began chattering about their ideas.

S s   T t   U u   V v   W

Every day that week as soon as school was out, the furry friends hurried to the woods to hunt for hat decorations. Gregory found shiny nuts. Mikey found green velvety moss. Gibby found bright berries and he tried hard not to eat them all. Payton didn't explore with the others. He made it very clear he already had the perfect hat decoration already picked out. "My hat is going to be a big surprise," he told everyone.

Mooki and his little friend Hannah decided they would shape hats from pond mud. They molded the hats to look like flowerpots, and when they were finished, they set them in the sun to "bake." When the hats were completely dry, they covered them with lots of big, colorful wildflowers. Then they tried on their creations.

"How charming you look, Mooki!" Hannah told the beaver and giggled.

"Not half as charming as you, Miss Hedgehog," teased Mooki, and he laughed right out loud.

That night Mooki invited Payton to sleep over with him at his house so they could both be on time for the start of the parade. Mooki put his mud hat on the front porch where he could get it first thing in the morning. He couldn't help wondering what Payton's hat, hidden away in Payton's backpack, looked like.

"Here's your perch," he told Payton, and then Mooki crawled into his own bed.

Payton jumped up on the perch and tucked his head under his wing. Just before he closed his eyes he thought, *My hat with its great big, gorgeous sunflower will be the best of all.* Then he went to sleep.

Payton didn't sleep very well. All night he squirmed and tried to get comfortable. He felt itchy all over and kept waking up on his perch. He scratched and scratched. *What could possibly be wrong with me? Must be the strange perch,* he decided.

The next morning Mooki woke Payton. "Good morning, Payton," he called. "How did you sleep?" Mooki didn't pay much attention as Payton grumbled about how awful he felt. Mooki went to the front porch to check on his hat.

Payton hopped down from his perch and went straight to the mirror to preen himself. He was so sleepy. When he finally opened his eyes enough to see himself in the mirror, he *screeched*, "I'm losing my beautiful feathers! Oh, my, what am I going to do? I can't let Mooki see me without my gorgeous feathers. I can't let *anyone* see me this way. I can't go to the parade with my feathers falling out! Oh, what shall I do? What shall I do?"

Out on the porch, Mooki was having his own troubles, "Oh, no! The porch is wet. Oh my! The path is wet. Oh, me! My hat is wet. It's *ruined!*" There on the porch was a big lump of mud—all that was left of Mooki's beautiful hat.

Now I don't have a hat for the parade, Mooki thought miserably. Well, at least he could still ride on the float, but what fun would that be without a hat to wear? His fun was spoiled. Mooki plopped down on a step and buried his face in his paws. He was sooooo sad.

Inside, Payton was rushing back and forth screeching. "Tape! I need tape! There must be some here someplace. Ah, here it is!" And he began taping feathers back onto his body. As soon as Payton taped one feather on, another would fall off. It would have been very funny if it had not been so sad. Payton couldn't work fast enough to cover all the bald spots. He looked ridiculous with feathers sticking out in all directions. Poor Payton. He didn't know what to do. For the first time in his life, he wasn't the most beautiful critter in Hedge Hollow.

"Mooki, help me!" Payton squawked at the top of his lungs.

The screen door opened slowly and Mooki came shuffling in, head down.

"Mooki, look! My feathers are falling off. I can't go out today. What happened to me? I'm not the most gorgeous creature in all the forest."

At that Mooki sighed and raised his head. He took a good look at Payton. "Wowsy!" said Mooki. "I believe you're molting."

"Molting?" Payton almost croaked it out. "What's molting?"

"It's all right, Payton," Mooki told him. "As peacocks get older, each summer they lose their feathers. It just means you're growing up."

"But I don't want to grow up. Not today, anyway. My feathers were the most beautiful feathers in the whole world!" sobbed Payton. "How can I face my friends looking like this? How can I ride in the parade?"

"It's OK," Mooki assured him. "The critters will understand."

"I don't know if they will care," said Payton. "I've been so proud of winning the spelling bee, of the beautiful hat I made for the parade today, and of my beautiful feathers, I haven't thought much about anyone else."

"Well, we're a sad pair," said Mooki. "I don't have a hat to wear and you don't have any feathers to wear. I guess we just can't ride on the float, unless… hey, wait a minute." Mooki ran to the place where Payton had perched last night. He was back in a minute with his paws full of beautiful feathers.

"Look, Payton. If you share your feathers, we can both have a wonderful hat to wear on the float. Let's hurry. Maybe if you're wearing a beautiful hat, no one will notice you don't have any feathers. Come on! We're in this together."

Now Payton's face was all smiles. "Nah, I'll wear my own hat. And I will be happy to share my feathers with you. Let's get busy!"

They worked quickly and before long, they had made a very special hat for Mooki to wear. When Mooki put it on, he felt like a king.

"Oh, Payton, thank you. Thanks for being so kind."

Payton smiled, "No problem, Mooki. It was your idea. All I did was lose all my feathers. Now let's hurry to the parade. Oh, by the way, Mooki, do you have a shirt I could wear to cover up my bald spots?"

"Sure!" Mooki said and grabbed a bright red shirt off a hook.

When Mikey saw Payton, he yelped, "Yikes! What happened to you?"

"My feathers fell off and I tried to tape them back on. It didn't work," Payton told him.

Gibby just couldn't help it. He started to giggle. "Tape? You tried taping your feathers back on? You know, Payton, some of us have nice thick fur that never falls off. We don't have to use tape!"

Mikey tried to hide a smile as he nudged Gibby and whispered, "Don't make him feel worse."

"Why not? He always brags and makes everyone else feel bad," Gibby said.

"Ah, guys," Mooki, told them. "Payton can't help it. He's molting." All the critters took a step backward. Mooki laughed. "It's all right. He's not contagious. It happens to birds. His feathers will grow back—eventually."

"Oh, I thought he had a terrible disease or something," said Mikey.

"He's got a disease, all right. It's called 'bragging disease,'" said Gibby.

Just then Miss Taylor stood up to announce the start of the parade. "Payton, I'm so sorry about your misfortune. I have to say, though, you look splendid in that red shirt."

Payton didn't strut and brag this time. He just smiled and said, "Thank you, Miss Taylor."

"Now to the rest of you, I want to say you did an incredible job on your hats. They *all* celebrate the beauty of nature. However, there is one hat that seems especially unique. Mooki, please join me and share with us how you made this beautiful hat. We've never before seen anything quite like it on a beaver."

The crowd clapped as Mooki joined his teacher. "First, I want to thank a special friend of mine for all his sharing and help. Payton gave me his feathers. Then he helped me make the hat. Thank you, Payton. Thank you from the bottom of my heart!"

Once again Payton said nothing. He just lowered his head. All the critters gasped in surprise. Why, Payton looked almost humble!

Finally the critters climbed on the float. It moved slowly down the street. Mooki looked splendid! He looked like royalty. The feathers that covered his head gleamed and sparkled like jewels in the sunlight. Mooki smiled and blushed.

Payton was thinking and thinking. *Gibby is right. I have been proud. I am always bragging and acting like I'm better than everyone else. I've been an awful, selfish critter. Well, I surely don't have anything to brag about now.*

Then Payton cleared his throat and took a deep breath. He had something important to say. All the critters turned to look at him. He said, "I'm so sorry for the way I've been acting. I know my bragging probably hurt many of you. I haven't acted like a friend at all. Well, I found out today what's really important is not about being the best at everything; it's about helping a friend. Will you all forgive me for being so proud?"

"Yes! Yes!" all the critters shouted. Mooki, Mikey, and Gibby crowded around Payton to give him a big hug. Then the critters turned to wave at the crowd and kept on waving right to the end of the parade. It was a very happy day.

Small Talk by Gary Smalley

Dear Parents,

Let me share with you one of the greatest secrets of life! Here it is: Everything good and honorable about ourselves, our children, and others, comes from God's goodness.

It's true, yet some of us forget this truth and think our accomplishments are due to our own abilities. We have a superior attitude and sometimes we even brag. Bragging is unhealthy. Why? Because God is the one who has given us all our gifts. When we brag, we are saying, "Look at me. Look at all my gifts. Look at all that I can do!"

We can teach our children to honor others by first setting an example of being appreciative of the skills, talents, and intelligence God has given us. God has given each of us the gifts he wants us to have. Those gifts are as individual as we are, and every gift is valid. We could brag about the wonderful gifts God has given us, but in reality they are not our gifts; they are his.

One of the gifts he gives us is the opportunity to value and serve others, and that can be very exciting. When you and your children recognize the value in others and serve them as people gifted by God, you are doing God's highest will. "Love your neighbor as you love yourself" (Matthew 22:39). An added benefit that comes when we validate the gifts of others, is that at the same time, we have the privilege of validating and cultivating our own gifts.

Before we can teach our children to value others, we parents must first admit that we don't value others the way we should. We need to ask God to help us. We need Christ to work in us and give us his power. Then we will be able to see others in the way God sees them. The Bible says, "God continues to give us more grace." [The inner power to do his will and to love others.] "God opposes those who are proud." [Those who think they are self self-made and can handle life without God.] "But he gives grace to those who are humble." [Those who humbly recognize that God made everything they have and that he alone gives the ability to love others.]" (James 4:6).

I'm reminded of the time a couple of young boys were bragging about whose dad was the greatest. They had a scuffle over it, one boy hit the other, and the neighbor boy ran home in tears. They were both very young, and they had not learned to love a "neighbor as themselves."

Pretty soon the neighbor woman came to the door, holding her young son's hand. The woman of the house answered the door, and after hearing what had happened, she quickly called her son to apologize. "Did you hit your friend?" she asked him.

"Yes," he said quietly.

"Son, do you have anything to say to your friend?" she asked.
No, he didn't have anything to say. Then she finally asked him, "Is there anything you want to do?"

"Yes," he answered loudly. ""I want to knock him on the ground!" His mother was embarrassed, to say the least.

Later, after the young boy had calmed down a bit, he and his mother were able to talk about the incident and pray together. He was able to admit that he had not done or said the right thing. He had not shown the right attitude toward his neighbor. They prayed together and she began to teach him how to cry out to God for his Spirit to enable him to love others.

In our story, Payton was a braggart. He hurt others by his bragging. He had not yet discovered the importance of seeing the gifts Mooki and others had. In this story he learns the importance of helping other forest creatures grow their own special gifts, instead of bragging about all his own. Payton finally learns that loving and serving others, is the greatest gift anyone can have.

I hope that as you read *Mooki and the Too-Proud Peacock* with your child, you'll encourage your child not to brag about how good he or she is. Use the ideas in SmallTalk to teach your child how to serve and love others.

After you've read *Mooki and the Too-Proud Peacock* with your child, ask these questions:

1. Why did Payton love to brag?

2. How did it make the other critters feel when they heard Payton bragging?

3. How did Payton feel when he lost all his feathers?

4. What did Payton do to make Mooki feel really special?

5. Have you ever bragged about something? What?

6. Rather than bragging, what are some ways in which you can show love to others?

7. What are some ways in which you can serve others?

"Don't do anything only to get ahead. Don't do it
because you are proud. Instead, be free of pride. Think of
others as better than yourselves" (Philippians. 2:3-4).